# Love Me in the Dark

## Hayley Briana

# <u>YOU CAN REPORT PIRATING</u>

Not many people are aware, but if you notice pirating of an author's work (or any pirating in general) you can report it anonymously to the FBI. As we have seen, they can take down a site for pirating.

Supporting these institutions makes you a thief. NO ONE IS ENTITLED TO SOMEONE ELSE'S WORK! Pirating is a crime and you can face large fines of up to $250,000 USD and jail time of 5 years.

If you can't afford the book(s), maybe try reaching out to the author directly. Many are willing to offer you a free download of their book. If you can't afford my books, that's perfectly fine and I'm happy to send you an eBook at no charge.
Also, joining an author's newsletter is a great way to stay up to date on any sales or freebies they have offered.

**To report pirating you can contact your local FBI Office and/or report online at**
https://www.ic3.gov/ **or** https://tips.fbi.gov/

*For those out there who have always wondered what it
would be like to fuck a ghost*

# CONTENT WARNING

Disclaimer: This book contains explicit content and dark themes that may be considered traumatic and offensive to some readers. Please check triggers before reading. If you are not comfortable with some of these topics, please put this book down and do not read it. This work of mature fiction is only for those 18 or older.

For a full list of triggers, please visit
HayleyBrianaWrites.com

*Scan to see a list of triggers*

# TABLE OF CONTENTS

# Chapter 1



I am fully aware that I'm running. Running from the only life I'd ever known. I was running from the man that I thought would be mine forever. I had done everything that a proper girl was meant to do, but it still ended me up in the hospital with broken ribs and a mass of bruises to show what love could do to people.

I didn't tell anyone where I was going. Just pulled as much money from my account as possible and high-tailed it out of there faster than a dog with a bone. I wasn't sticking around to see if the asshole would do it again. I'd given him years of my life. Thankfully, I hadn't been stupid enough to marry him.

I had no family or friends other than the ones that came with Drake. They weren't real friends. Friends wouldn't side with someone who had caused you to be laid up in the hospital attached to all manner of machines, broken bones, and a concussion that left your mind blank even after months of recovery.

I knew right then and there that I wasn't cared about in that stuffy town. Where everyone knew your business and still did nothing to help you out when you needed it most. I was grateful some part of me knew to put away money. It didn't take me long to go to the courts, file a restraining order, and then get the hell out of there. I'd even legally changed my name. I couldn't bring myself to change my first name, seeing it was my late mother's name, but the rest could go. I was no longer Brooke Williams, but Brooke Cooper. It would take some getting used to, but at least it wouldn't be too hard to figure out with time.

I'd managed to get across four state lines by the time anyone thought to contact me. All reaching out on Facebook, which I was going to delete as soon as I got settled in my place. No more social. Just a simple burner phone, a place to put up my boots, and I could deal with the rest of the crap later.

The town I ended up in was huge compared to the small town I'd grown up in. Living in a large city, even outside of it, had never been something I'd wanted. That made it the best place to run to. It was so out there for me that no one from my old life would suspect this was where I would end up. I'd spent a few days in a dingy motel until I could get an appointment to look at one of the few places I could afford to live, just outside of the city limits. Being stuck in the city wasn't something I wanted to do. I had a car and could use that to get around and do more in town once I got myself a job. That shouldn't be hard either. No one wanted to work for nothing anymore, but beggars can't be choosers. I wasn't interested in begging to get myself back on my feet. Until then, I had plenty left over after paying my rent for the next 6 months. I wasn't sure if I'd be staying here that long. Life was my oyster, as they say.

# Chapter 2



Today was my big move-in day. It made it easier that the place came fully furnished because my small little suitcase was shit. It would take me all of 5 seconds to walk through the door with everything I owned. Despite that, the weather was the perfect kind of day to curl up on a couch with a hot cup of coffee and a good book. For now, I had enough food and water to last me a few days.

It was a cold and rainy day in the middle of winter, and my newly healed bones ached. I wanted to blast the heaters and get comfy with my e-reader. The thing was a godsend since I couldn't even bring my book collection along for my new life. Oh well, I'd work on building it all up again soon.

I was trying to be optimistic as I slid the key into the door to the little one-bedroom, one bath cabin type home. It was the perfect size for me. Hey, maybe I'd adopt a cat or some shit, so I wasn't so lonely. The thought made me smile as I walked over the threshold. Everything was covered in a thick layer of dust, white sheets spread over the furniture as I took in the space.

"Honey, I'm home." I laughed at my joke, shutting and locking the door behind me as I went to uncover the furniture and get things scrubbed down. I might have nothing to my name except what could fit in my suitcase, but if I was going to be living in this place, I could at least keep it clean.

It had been an easy, yet tiring, day of cleaning. I'd blasted my favorite rock playlist on my phone as I scrubbed every surface until the place was spotless. Even though it was cold, I left the windows open, letting the place air out as I went about making sure I had everything I would need. I'd have to make a run to the store for a few things, but my throw blanket would work for now to keep the chill at bay.

I lay on the couch, music still playing, as I pulled my e-reader from my suitcase. Now was the time to rest and read. The only thing that could have made this better was a good, fluffy pillow and a cup of coffee.

I'd worry about that tomorrow.

# Chapter 3

## Phantom

I watched the redhead as she worked to clean up the place. Uncovering the small amount of furniture and scrubbing away the dirt and grime. Watching her was going to become my new favorite activity. I loved watching her ample breasts spill from the top of her tank top. How her flesh jiggled and moved with her. How her ass shook from side to side as she walked around the small space. So fucking hot. I felt myself grow hard, working my cock in my hands. How good would it feel to plunge into that warm, tight hole of hers? To feel something other than this damning cold.

It had been far too long since I'd known any sort of pleasure or warmth. When was the last time someone ever ventured into this house? Not since I'd been here, I think. It had been years. Maybe longer. It was hard to tell time now that there was no point in remembering. The last beings to stay here were a group of hunters who had stayed for a few days, but none caught my interest like this woman.

If I were being honest, there wasn't much that I did remember about my past. Just waking up here and my name.

I awoke just as I am right now.

Alone and cold. So fucking lonely.

But here was a plaything for me. I'd make sure that I had my fun with her for as long as she decided to stay.

I just sat and watched from the shadows as she finished cleaning and lay down on the couch. The way her body moved had my cock hard in my hand all day. I just wanted to touch her. To get a little taste. Could I taste her? I wasn't sure, but I wanted to find out.

She sat there scrolling on some sort of device while wrapped in a thin little blanket. It wasn't long before she'd fallen asleep and I took my chance. Slinking over to where she was sleeping deeply on the couch. I took my time moving the device from her hands to lie on the coffee table before pulling the blanket off her, revealing the treasure underneath. Before laying down, she'd changed out of her dirty clothes and slipped into an oversized t-shirt with nothing on underneath. From this angle, I could see her glistening cunt waiting for me to dive in for a taste. Her thick thighs spread just enough for me to fit between them as I inhaled the smell of her warm sex. She smelled divine. Like the air after a warm summer rain. So clean. So fresh.

I couldn't stop myself as I slid my tongue along her folds, her taste exploding on my tongue. I groaned, nearly coming on the couch beneath me, but I needed to be quiet. I didn't want her to wake up with me like this, but I couldn't stop myself. I lapped at her wet little cunt, her legs opening wider for me as a soft sound left her full lips. Looking up, she was still asleep. I needed her to stay that way.

I ate my fill until she was coming on my tongue, soaking the couch beneath her. I was so fucking hard I couldn't contain myself. As gently as I could, I positioned myself at her opening and thrust into her slowly as I felt her warmth surround my cock. She was so fucking warm. The only warmth I'd felt since waking up in this house. I took my time, sliding in and out of her slowly, trying not to move her much as I fucked her tight little cunt. It had been so long that in only a few thrusts into her warm sex, I came. Filling her greedy little cunt until my release was dripping from her onto the couch when I pulled out of her.

Still, she slept on, completely oblivious to the fact I'd just fucked her sweet little hole. I watched as more of my seed leaked from her. No, that wouldn't do. Slipping my fingers between her folds, I gathered as much as I could, pushing it back into her. A low groan left my lips as her pussy clenched around the digits. Soon, very soon, I would claim her while she was awake. I could just imagine her moans filling the small house as she came for me like a good little girl.

# Chapter 4

## Brooke

I have been here for about a week. Always having this sinking feeling that I was being watched. Nothing overly weird had happened since I'd arrived in the little cabin outside of town. The only weird thing to happen was that I woke up every morning soaking wet. It was almost as if I'd come in my sleep. I was sticky. Covered in my own fluids, and the couch was officially starting to smell like sex. I was sore between my legs and sated even though I hadn't so much as touched myself.

I found that insanely weird because it had never happened in the twenty-three years of my life. I'd never been the overly sexual type, not losing my virginity until I met my ex in high school. He'd been the only person I'd ever been with. While I'd done whatever I could so that he was happy, I was fine to go without. My thoughts spiraled as I thought about it all. It was probably just the stress and my body was acting out while I slept. That was a thing, right?

Well, that was enough thinking about that. Today I needed to go into town to get some things to make this place liveable and my own. I'd gone grocery shopping a few days ago at the biggest grocery store I'd ever seen in my life. Now it was time for the fun stuff. I got dressed quickly in a comfy sweater and leggings before heading out the door. Making sure to lock up as I was leaving.

That same feeling of being watched followed me until I was leaving in my car down the long driveway that cuts through the woods.

***

It had been a successful day of shopping. I'd finally gotten bedding so that I could sleep in a bed again. Everything was in shades of black and grey for simplicity. I wanted the place to seem like me even if I couldn't splurge too much. Everything was a necessity, with nothing too big that couldn't be thrown in the car if I needed to get out of dodge.

I did spend a bit extra on one of those fancy single-serve espresso machines. A good cup of coffee was a must, and I wasn't about to go without. I'd always wanted one and now was the perfect time to start doing things for myself.

I took my time setting everything up, cleaned the couch with some cleaner I had picked up, and sat down with a hot cup of coffee to read before heading to bed. I was just about to doze off when I felt eyes on me again. This shit was getting ridiculous.

I stood from my spot on my bed where I'd been reading, grabbing the baseball bat from the side of my bed as I walked over to the window. Nothing. It was completely silent out here. The only sounds from the wildlife that lived in the surrounding woods. I looked in the living area and the bathroom. I even walked around the property only to find nothing.

"Fucking hell Brooke. It's just all the stress. He's not going to find you here. Stop being such a fucking idiot." I wanted to slap myself for being so high-strung and worried that someone from my old life would find out where I was. I didn't even have dial-up out here. How the fuck was anyone going to know where I was?

I walked inside, locking the door and checking the windows before I called it a night. Maybe some sleep would help me start to feel normal again.

Walking over to my kitchen counter, I took out my sleeping meds. Without these, I'd found it impossible to get a decent night's sleep.

# Chapter 5

## Phantom

My new plaything was scared of something. I could tell simply by the way she was always looking over her shoulder, always alert when she wasn't sleeping. I'd been watching her earlier as she prowled around the house, swinging a baseball bat and muttering to herself.

She was scared someone was going to find her out there. Was she running from something or someone?

Anger ragged in me as I thought of anyone harming what was mine. She may not know that she belonged to me, but that did not negate the fact that she was mine. If anyone ever showed up here, they would never be seen again.

I sat there watching her as she crawled into bed, falling into a deep sleep. I'd had my fill of her since she'd arrived and I counted down the minutes until she was in a deep sleep for me to have my fun with her. I hoped that soon I'd be able to play with her when she was awake. I wanted to be rough with her. To rut into her like a wild animal as I truly fucked her. Her wet pussy was so fucking tight around me and I craved to feel it at all hours of the day. To feel her inner walls clutching at me, holding me there as if she couldn't get enough of my cock.

I waited patiently until I was sure she was asleep. She'd started wearing panties to bed, and I wanted to rip them off as I positioned myself between her thick thighs. My little plaything was plump in all the right places. I just wanted to grip onto the meaty flesh, to leave bruises so that she and the world knew she was mine. I wanted her so badly I ached.

Her t-shirt had risen over her ample stomach, showing just the underside of her massive breasts. Ever so gently, I lifted her shirt, exposing her pink, perky nipples to the cool night air. Dipping down, I took one of the peaks into my mouth. Sucking softly, letting my tongue and teeth work at her tender flesh. My other hand working the other, its size spilling from my large hands. Her breath quickened. Even in her sleep, she wanted me just as much as I wanted her.

Reaching between her thighs, I could feel how wet she was underneath the offending fabric of her panties. I wanted to rip them from her luscious hips, but I couldn't have her being scared. I slipped my fingers underneath the fabric, stroking her clit until her hips were grinding against me. So fucking responsive to me and I couldn't wait to sink into her. I was almost too big to slip into her. Even after all these days working her cunt to stretch around me, she was still so fucking tight. She had to be ready to take me. I didn't want to hurt her unless she begged me to. I plunged my fingers into her core, seeking that bundle of nerves within her as my thumb worked her clit. Her walls clenched around my fingers as I fingered her tight little hole.

It didn't take her long to come on my hand. Her juices squirted from her, making the most delicious wet sounds I'd ever heard. Whimpers and moans left her lips as she came for me, never waking.

How lucky was I that she was such a sound sleeping, my sweet little pet?

Before she could finish coming on my hand, I pushed the fabric to the side, exposing her to me as I slipped inside her perfect pussy. A light groan of pleasure left me as I slipped into her slowly, placing my hands on her large thighs to spread her legs further as I slid in and out of her. Her pussy strangled my cock as one orgasm morphed into another.

The feeling of her wrapped around me was enough to send me over the edge, filling her sweet cunt until it was leaking out as I continued to fuck her. I wasn't done with her yet. I'd never be done with her.

# Chapter 6

## Brooke

My god, my pussy was so fucking sore this morning. I'd woken up yet again covered in sticky wetness that had me jumping in the shower and stripping the sheets from the bed to throw in the wash. This was going to become a problem.

As I was drying off my legs, I gasped in a mix of shock and horror. It looked like there were large handprints on my legs. The bruises were fresh in purples and blues. The fingers were much too large to be my own. What the fuck was going on? I rushed to get dressed, searching the windows and doors to make sure that everything was locked from the night before. I started searching for anywhere that someone could hide and sat down on the couch, completely defeated as panic worked through my system. Could someone have gotten in and then locked up behind themselves?

Of course not, you idiot! I was the only one with a key to this place. There was only one door in and out. In the middle of my panic, I came up with an idea. What if I went out and got security cameras for the place? If only to prove to myself that I was alone out here.

I didn't sit around thinking more about it. Jumping up from the couch and rushing out the door. I was going to figure out what the fuck was going on. I was done playing a victim, even to my own damn mind.

***

Who knew that security cameras could cost so much? I took my time setting everything up around the house, one in each room and 3 outside, so that I had a view of everything. I spent the day cleaning and checking the video recordings on my phone.

I couldn't see anything even while I felt the chill of eyes on my back. I was starting to think I was being paranoid again. I was just worried about Drake or someone from my old life finding me. I was seeing things. I must have just hit my leg, right? I was just seeing things.

It was much harder to sleep tonight, even with my meds, as I thought about what could be happening to me. I felt like I was losing my fuckin mind. I lay in bed, tossing and turning, until my clock showed the night turning to morning. At about two in the morning,

I finally succumbed to exhaustion.

# Chapter 7

## Phantom

I knew I should have been more careful, but I just couldn't help myself. I had very little control over where my redheaded plaything was concerned. I'd fucked her harder last night than I'd intended. Fucking her tight little hole rougher, leaving my mark on her thighs, filling her greedy cunt until I was completely spent.

Of course, she noticed the hand prints I'd left on her delicate flesh. I'd enjoyed watching her walk around with me all over her, even though I could tell she was panicked. She'd left in a hurry and came back with bags full of cameras that she set up everywhere around the house. My pet was becoming aware of my presence in the space we shared. It brought a smirk to my lips as I thought about what the possibilities could be for us.

She tossed and turned in her bed until late in the evening. Her fear was apparent until she finally fell asleep. If my pet wanted a show, I'd give her one. I waited until I was sure she was sound asleep before slipping to the edge of her bed. Letting my fingers trail over her soft flesh and into her red, silken hair. I looked up towards the camera she'd placed in the room and smiled at it before climbing onto the bed between her legs, dipping my face between her thighs to breathe in her scent, taking my time to savor her as I licked at her bare pussy. So wet, so ready for me. I couldn't get enough of her taste on my tongue. It was the only taste I would ever crave again as I speared her with my tongue. Working her just the way I knew my pet enjoyed it. Her hips rocked against my mouth as light sounds of pleasure left her full, pink lips.

I needed more, moving my fingers to her clit to give her the added friction she needed. Her mummers and whimpers of pleasure feed my hunger. Her fingers found their way into my hair as she rode my face, arching further into my touch until she was coming undone on my tongue. I groaned as she soaked my mouth and the bed beneath her. Looking up, she was panting, her eyes half open as she fought to wake from her slumber.

With a smile on my face, I licked her one last time before I let my body fade into nothingness. It was perfect timing as she sat upright in the bed, as if startled. Looking around the dark room to see if she could see anything as her hand reached toward her core. Feeling how wet she'd become for me.

My dick ached. I hadn't had the chance to slip inside her warmth tonight, but I was certain it wouldn't be much longer until she was begging for me to fuck her.

# Chapter 8



I felt something. I was positive I had as I sat up in bed, looking around to see that the room was empty. Reaching between my thighs, I was soaked, a groan of frustration leaving me as I got up to strip the bed again. I was so tired of cleaning up after making a mess all over myself. I'd worry about it in the morning, throwing a spare sheet on the bed and crawling under my warm blankets to sleep.

I must have laid awake for hours and I knew that sleep wasn't happening. The sun was just breaking over the tree line, creating a soft glow of light in my small bedroom. I decided now was probably a good time to check the footage from the night before. I was still so wet, my core needy. Fuck, why was I so damn horny all of a sudden?

I opened the app that recorded from the cameras and worked my way through until I'd fallen asleep. For a few minutes, nothing happened, and I was sure I was going crazy. That is, until a large figure appeared out of nowhere. I couldn't turn my eyes away as the thing's eyes flashed an eerie green as it looked at the camera. Its hands slipped along my arms and into my hair before it crawled into the bed with me, laying down between my legs.

My inner walls clenched on nothing as I watched this *thing* lick me until I was grinding against him in my sleep. My hands slipped into his nearly silver hair as I arched my back. It wasn't long after that I noticed I'd started to wake up. The thing disappeared just before I sat up in bed.

I watched part of the video over and over again. My core aching for attention and I couldn't help but reach my hand between my legs under the blanket until I was full-on fingering myself. Oh god, I was so wet. Coming all over my fingers as I pleasured myself, watching whatever that thing was eating me out while I was asleep.

Something was seriously wrong with me, but I couldn't seem to shake the ache as I got up from the bed to clean myself off. I felt dirty, even though I felt an empty ache in my core for the rest of the day. I still couldn't wrap my head around what I'd seen or my reaction to it.

It was almost nightfall, and I didn't have any better grasp on my situation. I decided going to bed was probably the only thing I could do. So I dressed in an oversized t-shirt and crawled into my bed. Again struggling to relax enough to sleep. I tossed and turned, not even the slightest bit tired, until I felt my anger rising. Sitting up in bed, I looked around the room, still seeing nothing.

"Alright, asshole. Show yourself. I know you're here somewhere. I can feel you fucking watching me."

Great, now I was talking to ghosts like an idiot. I really had lost my mind. The longer I sat there, nothing showed itself, until I was thinking about maybe admitting myself into some sort of institution. Maybe the beating I'd taken from Drake had messed me up more than the doctors thought. Maybe I was just going crazy because of the trauma.

I was about to just give up and lay back down until the bedroom door opened on its own. I still saw nothing as the door shut again. Clenching the sheets on my bed as fear took over and my heart beat faster.

What the fuck was this thing? I sat perfectly still, my eyes looking around the room for any sign of something in the darkness.

Nothing moved, and I was sure I'd been holding my breath this whole time. I was losing my damn mind. At least, that's what I thought until I felt an icy breath on my neck.

"Hello, my pet." It purred in a deep voice as my body broke out in chills, my pussy clenching around nothing.

Fuck me, it sounded so hot with that deep husky voice. I clenched my thighs together as my core pulsed. Yep, losing my mind.

"Who are you? What are you?" I asked in a rush as the covers were tossed from my legs. Shivers racked my body. I could stop this. I could get the hell out of here and never look back. It hadn't been the first time I'd run, but I was so curious, so needy.

I felt as long fingers trail up my bare legs. They were so cool to the touch. "None of that matters, pet. All that matters is that I taste you."

At those words, I felt its hands wrap around my ankles, pulling me to lie down as it spread my legs, taking a place between them. The bed dipping as its large body rested between my thighs, a cool breath against my pussy. Oh god. What was happening?

A moan slipped from my lips as I felt a cold tongue lick me from my clit to my entrance, plunging into me at a quick pace. On instinct, I reached between my legs, shocked, as my fingers slid through a head of hair. The thing didn't stop its tongue as it ate at me, consuming me. My fingers gripped onto the hair I couldn't see as I chased my release. This thing knew what it was doing. I was already so close. Oh my god, what was I doing?

My heart raced as I ground against that mouth I couldn't see but could feel. His fingers found my clit to work me into a frenzy as my world crashed around me. I'd never come so hard in my life and it just kept going as the thing between my legs licked and sucked at me. I was panting as it moved away from me, a whimper slipping from me at the loss.

The loss of contact didn't last long as I felt a large body rest atop mine. Something hard and big pressing against my entrance, "What are you..."

I couldn't get the words out as it pushed itself into me, stretching me wider than I'd ever been stretched. My back arched at the intrusion. A gasp left me as it filled me completely. Oh god, it was so big. I couldn't tell where pain and pleasure ended and began as it moved inside of me. My hips worked to match the thrusts as it picked up its pace. I was going to come again.

Looking down, I saw my pussy stretching around nothing. It was the hottest thing I'd ever seen until I was coming all over it, my release shiny over the thing that was fucking me. It didn't stop, only fucking me harder and faster. As it fucked me, it groaned and growling out in pleasure. Taking me to new heights as it plunged into me, my head falling back and eyes rolling into the back of my head as I raced towards another orgasm. My fingers reached for something to grab onto and I was surprised when my hands wrapped around muscular forearms. I could feel the muscles and veins of this thing. It felt so human. My thoughts stalled as I screamed out another release. Its groans of pleasure filled the room. I could feel it pulsing inside of me, filling me up as we came together.

My mind was blank as I felt it slide from me, leaving me feeling empty, sated, and so tired. I gasped to catch my breath as I lay there in my bed. I no longer felt it touching me while I came down from my high. I nearly jumped when I felt something cold at my entrance. Looking down to see the faint outline of a man between my legs, his fingers dipping into the come leaking from me, pushing it back in. My eyes shot up towards a pair of green, glowing eyes as it pushed its come back into me, fingering me slowly with its long fingers until I was tossing my head back to moan again. This was so fucked up. Did I seriously just let a ghost fuck me?

But I didn't care. I couldn't care about anything else as it brought me to another blinding orgasm. I was coming around his fingers so fast. Oh god, I'd never come so much in my life. I was exhausted as it pulled the covers back over my chilled body.

This is just some fucked up dream, I thought as my world turned dark.

# Chapter 9

## Brooke

I woke up with a start. Covered in sticky dried come and the events of the night before flashed through my mind. I wanted to scream, but another part of me wanted to do it again. It had to be a dream. There was no way any of that actually happened.

I pulled out my phone just to check, a moan slipping from my lips as I watched something invisible fucking me into oblivion. I watched it over and over again. Unsure of what I was seeing, even though I'd lived through those moments. Felt its icy touch on my skin. Just the thought left me horny and my heart racing. I wanted this. I didn't even know what that thing was, but god it felt so good.

I was definitely losing my fucking mind. I showered, got dressed, and rushed out of the house. I needed to know what the hell was going on. I drove straight to the city library, searching for any information about the house I was now living in. Trying to see if this had happened to anyone else. I found nothing. There was nothing. No one had lived in that house for over 30 years. The last known residence renting the place out here and there, sort of like a B&B of some kind, usually to hunters who would use the land during hunting season. But it had been empty. Prior to that, there had been one owner. An older gentleman, Clint, and his son, Zane. There had been a string of murders in the area around that time. Young women had gone missing and their bodies were later found in the surrounding woods. They suspected the man, but only arrested him following the murder of his son in the small cabin.

My blood ran cold as I read through all the articles, looking over the crime scene photos of the 21-year-old Zane. The father had claimed that the son had been responsible for all the disappearances. That he'd killed his son to save the young women. The officers had never believed him since he'd killed his son in the same way as the women.

My heart raced. What if this thing was why those girls went missing? What if I'd just fucked some sort of murder? But he hadn't hurt me. That didn't seem right. I printed out the articles before heading back out to the house. Maybe that thing could give me some answers.

# Chapter 10

## Phantom

I couldn't get my pet off my mind all day. She'd accepted me last night, and all I wanted was to do it again and again. Her nails dug into me as I fucked her. Fucked her until she was exhausted from the pleasure I gave her. My cock was already hard, and I wrapped my hand around it, stroking lazily as I waited for my pet to get back. I couldn't wait to taste her again. To hear her scream out in pleasure for me like she'd done last night.

She walked into the room with a purpose. Tossing her bag on the floor as she slammed the door behind herself. Her eyes looked around the room, searching, but she wouldn't see me unless I allowed it. Her long red hair was tied up into a bun on the top of her head and she was dressed in a pair of black leggings and a dark green sweater. My dick hardened at the sight of her as her booted feet stomped along the hardwood floors.

So much anger and passion radiating off of her. It made her even more breathtaking. Again my hand reached down to wrap around my cock, fisting it in my hands as I stroked myself where I sat in a corner chair.

"Alright, whatever you are? Show yourself. I'm sick of playing this fucked up game." She said, anger lacing her angelic voice.

With a smirk on my face, I let myself materialize where I was sitting, still stroking my cock as I watched her. As soon as she noticed me, her eyes dropped to watch the action, her lips parting, breaths turning into pants. I could feel the heat radiating from her from here as she watched me pleasure myself.

"Do you like what you see, pet?" I asked, my voice gone gravely as I watched her reaction.

Her eyes shot up to mine and her pupils were blown wide with lust as she tried to look anywhere except where my hand was jacking off my hard cock. "You're human?"

Her question had me stilling my hand for a moment before continuing my teasing. "I used to be."

She took a tentative step towards me, swaying on her feet slightly. "So you're a ghost?"

I rubbed my cock faster, tilting my head back to focus on the pleasure, wishing it were her warm cunt or mouth. "Yes."

My response came out in a hiss as I worked my shaft. Moving my hand faster. I almost didn't notice that she was now standing directly in front of me, her eyes fixed on my hand and cock again. "Suck it."

Her eyes became hungry at my words. It didn't take her long to drop to her knees and take me into her mouth and hand. I was far too big to fit down her throat, her mouth stretched to its limit around my cock as she sucked and licked the length. I fisted her hair, thrusting up into her, causing her to gag as I pushed into her throat.

Her mouth was so hot, so wet, and I couldn't help myself as I fucked her face. Groans of pleasure left me as I forced myself down her throat, her gagging causing her throat to clench around my cock as I filled her. Looking down to watch her take my cock, I was so turned on by the tears leaking from her eyes, streaming down her plump cheeks, her nails digging into my thighs. I gave her no control. Just fucked her until I was spilling down her throat.

"Swallow it all, pet," I groaned as I emptied into her waiting mouth.

She did as she was told, swallowing every drop and licking me clean. She pulled away from me, her lips creating a loud pop as my cock was freed from her mouth. I gripped her hair in my hand, forcing her to look up at me as I bent to claim her lips in a searing kiss. Warmth spread through every spot where we touched.

She moaned against my lips, pulling me closer to deepen the kiss.

"Mine," I whispered when she broke the kiss to breathe. Taking in deep lungfuls of air.

# Chapter 11



I couldn't catch my breath. I had just let a ghost fuck my mouth, and I'd enjoyed every second of it. I must be fucked in the head because I was so fucking wet. If it weren't for my panties and leggings, I'm sure I would be sitting in a puddle right now. He was so damn cold to the touch as he kissed me, pulling my hair so that I was exactly where he wanted me.

"Mine." He growled against my lips.

That single word sent a shock to my core as I clenched my thighs together. How could one word have me melting right here on the living room floor? I seriously needed someone to take some scans of my brain because nothing about this situation should be possible.

Thoughts of what I'd found today came roaring back into the forefront of my brain. I stood from my spot on the floor and walked over to get the papers out of my bag. Turning to him again, I took in his appearance. Pale, almost white skin, silver hair that was short on the sides and long in the front, glowing green eyes that were completely unnatural but still left me weak in the knees, abs, and muscles for days, and my god he was still fucking hard. His dick was fucking huge, and I wanted to feel it inside of me again.

Damn it, focus, Brooke!

I walked over, holding the article up for him to see. It was the one about the missing girls and what Clint had said. "Did you do this?"

He shrugged as he looked over the article. "I don't know."

Anger boiled in my gut at his nonchalant tone. "What the hell do you mean, you don't know?"

"I don't remember my life. Just my name. I'd rather not talk about this, pet. I'd much rather sink my cock into your wet pussy."

How could he be this way? Was that all he thought about? I mean, I wasn't much better as I looked down at his cock again. God, I wanted to fuck him, but I was still so mad. I threw the papers into his face as I turned my back and stormed off into my room, shutting and locking the door behind me as I went.

# Chapter 12

## Phantom

I glared at the door as it was slammed shut behind her. While I was annoyed that she hadn't taken me up on the offer to fuck, I enjoyed watching her plump ass bounce as she stormed off. She was going to be fun to play with.

I let her be for a moment, letting my form fade as I made my way into her room. She was stripping the dirty sheets from the bed, muttering to herself as she went about her cleaning. She was annoyed by something and I wasn't sure what to do. I thought she wanted the same things I did. For me to bring her unlimited amounts of pleasure. It was clear that she wanted me, so what was the problem?

After she'd finished making the bed, I walked over to stand behind her, brushing my lips over her exposed neck, gripping onto her hips to pull her back flush against me. A gasp left her lips, followed by a moan, when I sucked her tender flesh into my mouth.

"What are you doing?" Her voice was soft and filled with hunger as I slid a hand around her front, down her pants to slide my fingers along her wet folds. She moaned at my touch as I plunged my fingers into her needy little cunt.

"Oh, god." She moaned out breathlessly as I stroked her faster, forcing my fingers as far as they would go.

"That's it, my pet. Come on my fingers like a good little girl." Her fingernails dug into my arm as I continued to stroke her until she was coming with an audible curse.

I slipped my fingers from her warm center, bringing them to my lips to taste her release, growling at the taste as she tensed against my front, "So fucking warm and all mine."

She whimpered as I released her. She stumbled a moment before fixing her clothes and taking a seat at the end of the bed. Her eyes scanned the room in search of me until I let myself be seen. Her eyes zeroed in on my hard cock again. The thought that she wanted me fueled my hunger as I walked up to her. I was in the perfect position to thrust into her waiting mouth again, but held back my need to find out what she wanted from me.

I gripped her chin, forcing her brown eyes to look into my own. "Now tell me, what is bothering you, pet?"

"You can't tell me anything about yourself. You could be a homicidal ghost for all I know." She was nearly shrieking. I wrapped my hand around her throat, holding her in place as I felt her heart race against my fingers.

"My name is Zane. I woke up here, and I've been trapped within the borders of the property since then. I would never hurt you, Brooke. I would do everything in my power to make sure that you are safe."

Her eyes widened, breath catching in her throat, and I could feel her heart beating faster. "Have you been watching me this whole time?"

"Yes." I wasn't going to lie to her. If nothing else she deserved the truth from me.

"Were you fucking me in my sleep? Was that why I always woke up a mess?" Her breathing was turning into gasps. She was breathless as she spoke.

"Yes," I growled out, wanting to claim her right here, right now.

Her eyes searched mine, her pupils dilated to take up the brown of her iris as she looked up into my face. "Do it again."

I smiled wickedly at her as my hand tightened around her throat. With my other hand, I reached between her, ripping the thin material of her pants and panties to give me access to her wet cunt.

With my hand still wrapped around her throat, I forced myself between her legs, plunging into her warm depths as her inner walls tightened around me. "So fucking wet and warm for me."

She moaned out, moving her hips to meet mine as I fucked her so hard that her breasts were bouncing underneath her shirt and I wanted to take the round globes into my mouth. To taste her warm flesh as she came apart beneath me. It would have to wait for another time because I wasn't about to leave the warm heat of her body. I reached between us as I fucked her, rubbing her clit to give her exactly what she needed until she came around me, soaking my cock and the edge of the bed. My name tumbled from her lips as her orgasm overtook her. At the sound, I came inside her greedy pussy, filling her to the brim.

# Chapter 13

## Brooke

I'd never wanted something so much in my life. I couldn't even keep track of how many times I'd begged him to make me come. He was so good at it and I couldn't get enough. I was sore and thoroughly fucked at this point as I lay in bed, Zane's powerful arms wrapped around me. I enjoyed being able to feel his cool skin against my own. He was a ghost, so it made sense that he wouldn't feel warm. He also didn't have a heartbeat and didn't breathe, which I noticed as soon as I laid my head on his chest.

I tried not to think about it too much. If all of this was in my head, it was a pleasurable dream for now. I felt sated and happy for a moment. We lay in each other's arms, just talking after he'd made me come until I was seeing stars in my vision. He'd wanted to know everything about me, holding me close to his side as I told him about my life before coming here. Even telling him everything that had happened with Drake and why I'd run away.

"If he ever comes here, I'll take care of him. He will never lay another finger on you again, my pet." He'd meant every word as anger was apparent in his tone. I didn't want to know what he had in mind. I didn't care, as he placed a gentle kiss on the top of my head.

How odd was it that I had found something like this with a hot-as-hell ghost, of all things? That thought swirled in my mind as I drifted off to sleep.

***

I woke up to the feeling of a tongue lapping at my entrance, a moan slipping from my lips as my hands found their way into Zane's hair.

"Please Zane, don't stop," I begged, riding his face as his tongue plunged into my pussy.

A girl could get used to waking up like this. He fucked me with his tongue until I was arching off the bed in pleasure, my orgasm ripping through me as I came apart on his tongue. He shouldn't have been so damn skilled at that. Zane always made me come so quickly. I'd always thought that I was just complicated. Drake said it was nearly impossible to make me come. I'd only ever come a few times with him when he'd fingered me, and it had been nothing like this.

My sex drive had skyrocketed. I couldn't get enough of Zane's icy touch. He was always ready to go for me. We spent weeks just wrapped up in each other. He no longer disappeared, staying in an almost human-like state so that I always knew where he was and could touch him. He could disappear at will, touch things, or go right through them. For me, he'd remained as human as possible, the only indication that he wasn't being his unnatural silver hair, glowing green eyes that watched me with the same hunger I was feeling, and how cold he was to the touch.

We fell into a routine, spending the days together unless I had to venture into town for food and anything else we needed. I'd finally had someone come by to set up a landline and internet and it was fun showing everything to Zade. Since he had no memories of his past life, it was as if he were seeing it all for the first time. Then again, if he'd been here for 50 years, I'd imagine that he hadn't had any of this stuff before.

"Can you get me pregnant?" The thought had been weighing heavily on my mind the past few days with all the sex we'd been having. I wasn't on any sort of birth control and wasn't sure how to even explain getting knocked up by a dead guy.

"I don't believe so, I am dead after all," he shrugged as he rubbed my feet while we lounged on the couch watching a movie. With having internet it made sense to get a tv too.

I thought it over with a smile on my face. "I guess that's why you don't taste like anything."

He smirked at me, wrapping his hand around my ankle to pull me down on the couch, his head dipping between my legs, pulling at the fabric of my panties with his teeth. "But you taste heavenly, pet."

His hand slipped up my legs towards my core, ripping the fabric so that I was bare for him. How many pairs of clothes was he going to ruin? I didn't have that much.

"You're going to make me have to buy more clothes if you keep doing that." I pouted, hoping my voice didn't sound as shaky as I felt.

He simply smiled up at me from between my legs, eyes shining as he looked up at me, "Then don't wear anything at all."

My face heated as he dipped his head again, running his tongue along my folds before diving in. Feasting on me as if he were a starved man. My hands slipped into his hair as I moaned out in pleasure. I'd never get tired of his wicked tongue, fingers, and cock.

# Chapter 14

## Brooke

I'd finally decided that I needed to get a job. While I had plenty of money left, I didn't want my savings to get too low. Zane wasn't happy about me being gone so much, but with a few blow jobs and lots of kinky sex, it had been easy to change his mind. There was a little diner right as you got into the city that had hired me and I worked early morning shifts 5 days a week. The pay wasn't the best, just above minimum wage, but it was enough to have me satisfied and included tips. I enjoyed the work and getting to meet new people, either those who worked in the city or were just passing through.

For the first time in my life, I was perfectly happy and content. I had someone at home waiting for me, who gave a shit, and a job where I could have some interaction with people who were still breathing. I couldn't believe the turn my life had taken. My smiles had become real, and I was finally feeling like a whole person again.

Everything was going perfectly until it wasn't. I was working a shift when a familiar F-250 pulled up out front of the diner during one of my shifts. The stickers on the windows marked it as exactly who I thought it was. I told my manager I was going to go clean up the back before leaving for the day. My heart raced as I rushed behind the doors to the kitchen. I washed dishes and clocked out as fast as I could, slipping out of the back where my car was hidden from the customers of the diner.

How the fuck had he found me so soon? I'd been so careful. My heart raced as I made my way home. I was in a panic as I walked through the door, locking every lock on the thing as I rested my forehead against the cold wood. A felt Zane approach me from behind without having to look. My eyes closed as I tried to focus on calming breaths. Zane's icy fingers brushed over my arms, soothing my racing heart.

"Pet, what's wrong?" Concern was evident in his voice as he pulled me back into his arms.

I turned to face him, embracing the cold that radiated from him as he held me. "He's here. He found me."

"Don't worry about him. He will never touch you again." Zane's arms tightened around me, grounding me. I knew he'd keep me safe.

***

I called out of work for the rest of the week. I didn't want to risk Drake finding me and prayed that he was just passing through and that he'd be gone soon. I didn't understand how he'd gotten so close. My body was tense. I was always checking the outdoor cameras to make sure that he wasn't outside.

Zane said nothing, only offering me company and distraction, which I was thankful for. I wasn't sure he could protect me if Drake showed up, but he reassured me that if he came here, I'd never have to worry about him finding me again.

Every part of me was aching to run. To get as far away from her as fast as I could. I couldn't do it though. How could I just leave Zane here, all alone? He wasn't able to leave, only able to venture a little way into the woods that surrounded the house. I had no choice but to stay because I couldn't just take him with me or leave him. He'd become a big part of my life and I couldn't do that to him. I'd grown to care for him since coming here and getting to know one another. This was the most stable relationship I could have ever imagined. Now that I thought about it, what exactly were we? Was this a relationship?

***

Three days. I had been locked in this house for three days with Zane, worshiping me until shit hit the fan. I was startled awake at the sound of a truck pulling up outside, and pulled the phone up to see Drake's truck as he cut the engine. Glancing around the dark room, Zane was already making his way out of the room. His eyes shone bright with rage when he looked over at me sitting up in bed.

"Pet, stay in this room, lock the door, and don't come out for anything. I'll get in when this dumb fuck is taken care of."

I wasn't going to argue with him. Locking the door as he disappeared through it. I sat on the bed, watching the video from my phone as Drake looked around the front of the house. He knocked on the front door and I pulled the covers tighter around myself, eyes glued to the screen as I watched, holding my breath.

"Brooke, open up. I know you are in there, baby. Come out so that I can take you home." I heard Drake pleading through the door and over the sound coming from the phone.

Without any warning, the front door opened, and Drake walked into my house. My blood ran cold as I switched to the camera in the living room. I watched in horror as he walked in towards my room, looking around. Had Zane let him in? I muted the volume on my phone as I listened to the footfalls of my ex making his way closer to my door. The air grew colder. I could see my breath in front of my face as I gasped quietly. Tears ran down my face and terror took over. I was going to die. If he opened that door, I was as good as dead.

Everything was silent as the footsteps stopped in front of my door. The handle wiggled.

"Baby, let me in. I'm so sorry for what happened, please just. What the fuck? Who are you?" I heard a struggle, reaching for my phone again as Drake fought off something in the hall. A scream filled the silence as I watched Drake being dragged across the wooden floor and out the door. I watched on the camera as he was pulled into the dark forest surrounding the property.

I sat there in bed, listening to the screams, until it became deathly quiet. A shiver worked its way up my spine as I sat there, waiting, with my phone clutched in my hands. It was so quiet, and I held my breath while scrolling through all the cameras. Nothing was making a sound outside and all I could hear was my pounding heart in my ears.

I felt like I sat there forever until I watched Zane drift into the room through the door. He was covered in blood. It dripped down his pale skin in the dim moonlight and I signed in relief that he was back with me. I didn't give a shit what he'd done to Drake as I lurched from the bed, colliding with Zane's solid form as I pulled his lips down to mine.

# Chapter 15

## Zane

I was still covered in that idiot human's blood when Brooke flung herself into my arms. Her lips were warm as she kissed me with a hunger and desperation I'd never felt from her. She was frantic as she tore off her clothes, pulling me back towards the bed where I followed her lead. At that moment, all I wanted was to feel her warmth surrounding me.

"Please, fuck me, Zane." She begged breathlessly.

I didn't have to be told twice, pushing her onto the bed, causing her body to bounce on the mattress as I placed myself above her, fitted between her thick thighs as I slid inside her warm center. She moaned as I captured her lips, rocking my hips at a hard, torturously slow pace as she clawed at my back.

My little pet always wanted more, and I gave her exactly what she needed. Moving my hips faster until I was fucking her so hard she was nearly hitting her head on the headboard. I couldn't get enough of her as she screamed out, soaking us in her release while I fucked her through it.

"Oh god, Zane, don't stop," she moaned towards the ceiling.

We were both covered in blood now and the sight of her like this had me feral for my pet. I fucked her that night until we both couldn't move. Staying deep inside her warm cunt as she gasped for breath. I placed light kisses over her full breasts, up her neck, and on her plump lips.

"Mine," I growled, pushing deeper into her.

"Yours," she moaned.

Such a good fucking girl, my little pet was. She'd been sent to me in my time of darkness. Made to love me in the dark.

# ALSO BY HAYLEY BRIANA

Angel of Blood

**COMING SOON**
Angel in Chains (A Hellfire Novella 2)
A Hellfire Novella 3
Fall From Grace
Fall to Sin
A Darkside Fairytale Book 1
A Darkside Fairytale Book 2

# ABOUT THE AUTHOR

Hayley Briana is a small-town girl from North Carolina, currently residing in Colorado. As a stay-at-home mom & wife, she needs some major self-care in the form of a good cup of coffee (or wine) and a good book. Escaping into a world of fantasy is Hayley's favorite pass time outside her day-to-day responsibilities. When she's not adulting or writing, you can most likely find her tucked away in her home library.

For more info on Hayley and what she is working on please visit HayleyBrianaWrites.com

Follow Hayley on Social

Instagram.com/hbrianawrites

TikTok.com/@beautyandthebookcase